The Adventures of Rosie Hart

For Lillian

For always being
my rainbow

A catalogue record for this book is available from the National Library of New Zealand.

ISBN 978-0-473-59687-3 (softcover), 978-0-473-59688-0 (softcover POD), 978-0-473-59690-3 (e-book)

Unicorn Mission

Iveta Ongley

Have you read the first two books in
The Adventures of Rosie Hart series?

Fairy Quest

Rosie's enchanting encounter with fairies turns into a dangerous adventure. Can she help to save fairy babies before it's too late? Will she succeed or perish on this quest?

Mermaid Rescue

Rosie is looking forward to some fun in the sun. But danger lurks beneath the surface of the sea. A sorcerer has cast a terrible spell over the Mermaid Princess, and Rosie is the only one who can save her. Together with her dragon friend, she has to follow the trail of dark magic and face the perils ahead.

Contents

Chapter 1

Magical Rainbow

Rosie woke up and listened to the rain pitter pattering on the roof of their house. She was in a grim mood. It was the start of her autumn school holidays, but she didn't look forward to them. Mum and Dad had to work so they couldn't go anywhere, and all her friends from school went away. With the rain arriving, even the fairies would be hiding in their tree to stay dry. And the worst was that Spark, her dragon friend, had gone to visit the mermaids. She was alone. What a horrible holiday this was going to be.

Rosie had a secret. She was friends with fairies and mermaids. She had enjoyed many magical adventures over the past few months. When they moved into their house, she discovered a tree full of fairies in her own backyard. While adventuring with the fairies, they saved a young dragon who had become Rosie's best friend. Together, they spent the summer holiday at the seaside where they helped to save a mermaid princess from an evil sorcerer.

Rosie let out a deep sigh, sat on her bed, wondering what to do with the day. She stood up and walked to the window. Pulling the curtain aside, she gasped. There, in the middle of the meadow, rose the biggest, brightest rainbow she had ever seen. The rain fell slowly but steadily and there was no sun peeking through the dark clouds. Rosie didn't understand how there could be a rainbow, especially such a beautiful one. She got dressed in a hurry and ran downstairs.

"Mum! Did you see the rainbow outside?" Rosie exclaimed.

"No, I didn't. It's raining too much for a rainbow, I would think," answered Rosie's mum.

"I know!" said Rosie. "But there is a rainbow in the middle of the meadow. Look!" Rosie took her mum's arm, dragging her to the window.

"I don't see any rainbow, Rosie. Where is it?" said Rosie's mum, confused.

"Right there!" stressed Rosie. And then

it hit her. Her mum couldn't see the rainbow, because it was magical.

"I'm going to have a look," declared Rosie, grabbing her rain jacket and gumboots.

Rosie shot out of the back door, ran through the garden, and pushed the gate at the back open. She sprinted across the field to the meadow beside the forest. While running, she glanced towards the tree where the fairies lived, but the tree stood still.

Rosie arrived at the rainbow, panting. It stretched from a little pond at the back of the meadow over the forest and far into the distance. Rosie marvelled at the bright colours.

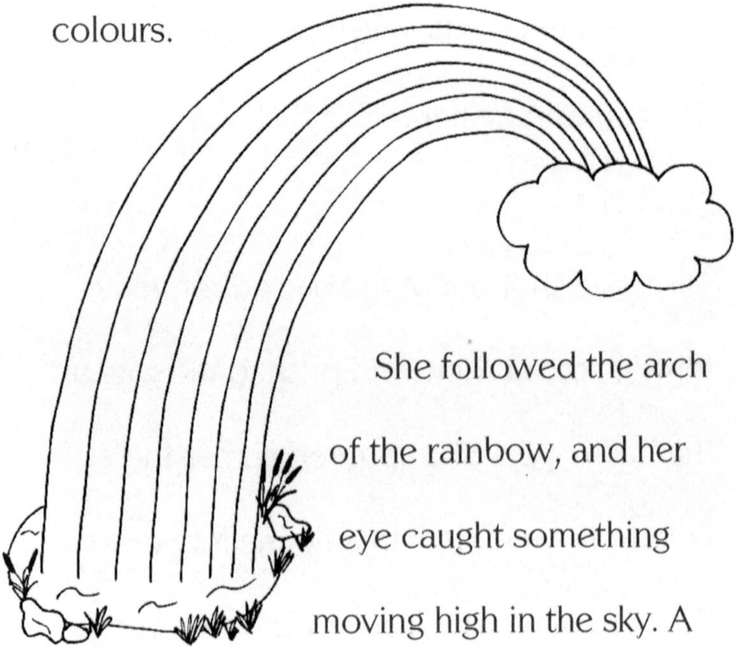

She followed the arch of the rainbow, and her eye caught something moving high in the sky. A little dot got bigger and bigger as it came nearer. Something was falling down towards Rosie. Then she heard a loud squeal.

“Wheeeee!” the sound rang happily and all of a sudden, a small, pale pink, unicorn with a rainbow-coloured mane dropped into the grass beside her.

Chapter 2

Unicorn Guardians

Rosie jumped with surprise. "Where did you come from?"

"I slid down the Rainbow," giggled the unicorn. "Who are you? My name is Stardream," she added.

"I'm Rosie. I live in the house over

there."

"Nice to meet you, Rosie. The fairies said that you would be here sooner or later. Apparently, you cannot keep your nose out of anything magical," laughed Stardream.

"Did they say that?" Rosie wasn't sure if she should be pleased or offended.

"Do you want to slide the rainbow, too?" the unicorn offered.

"Of course, I do! Can I? How?" Rosie blurted. "I don't have any magical powers."

"You don't need magical powers for that. You just have to believe." With that,

Stardream ran up the rainbow with lightness in her steps.

Rosie watched her, feeling at a loss. I just have to believe, she thought. Well, I do believe in magic, but will that be enough?

Rosie touched the rainbow and her hand went straight through. It was like touching air. She felt no sensation on her skin, no change of temperature or humidity. It wasn't solid and there was no way it was going to hold her. She looked wistfully at Stardream running there and back without problems.

"Remember! You have to believe!"

Stardream called down at her.

Rosie tried again. She closed her eyes and imagined herself climbing up the rainbow. With her eyes still closed and arms outstretched, she stepped forward.

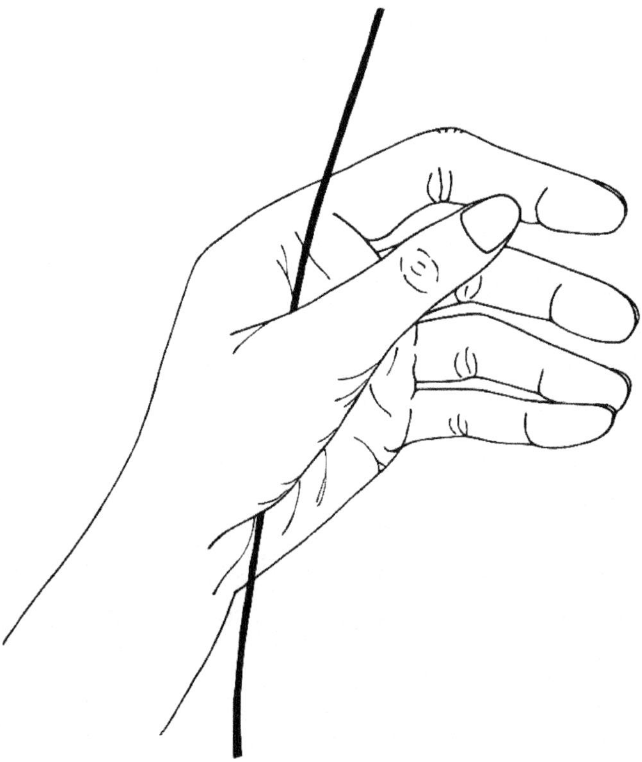

Her hand touched something smooth. She opened her eyes with surprise. She was touching the rainbow!

"I do believe," she told herself while getting a hold of the edge of the red strip. She pulled her body up. It was as if an invisible power was pushing her. It took little effort to climb to where the unicorn was waiting for her.

"I'm standing on a rainbow!" she told her with zeal.

"Let's slide," Stardream winked at her in mischief. She folded her back legs underneath her, and with a loud and happy whinny, sped away.

Rosie rushed after her, excitement building in her body. Thud, she landed on the grass.

"This was so much fun. I want to go again and from higher this time," Rosie exclaimed.

The two of them slid many more times, and their squeals of happiness echoed through the meadow.

"What do you two think you are doing!" boomed a voice from the field.

Rosie and Stardream stopped halfway up the rainbow and looked down.

"Uh oh, now we are in trouble," sighed the unicorn, staring at a group of unicorns with a large shining stallion at the front. "Come and meet my dad, Rosie."

They slid down, their happiness at once extinguished.

"Stardream, the Sacred Rainbow is not a playground. You were told to guard it, not to play on it," the unicorn's voice thundered.

"I'm sorry, Dad," Stardream mumbled. "I noticed Rosie coming, and I wanted to show off."

"Rosie? Are you Rosie?" the unicorn leader turned towards Rosie. She nodded slowly.

"Nice to meet you!" he exclaimed. "We've heard so much about you. You are one amazing young lady, aren't you?"

Rosie blushed and glanced at Stardream, who was looking pretty smug.

"I knew he would forget about me because of you," she whispered.

"Come, Rosie. You can tell me all about your adventures," urged the unicorn. "My name is Silvercrest and I am the leader of the Guardians of the Sacred Rainbow."

Rosie followed Silvercrest in the direction of the fairy tree.

"And I didn't forget about you, young lady. I'll deal with you later," he added toward Stardream. Rosie saw her smile fading as she walked after them with her head hanging low.

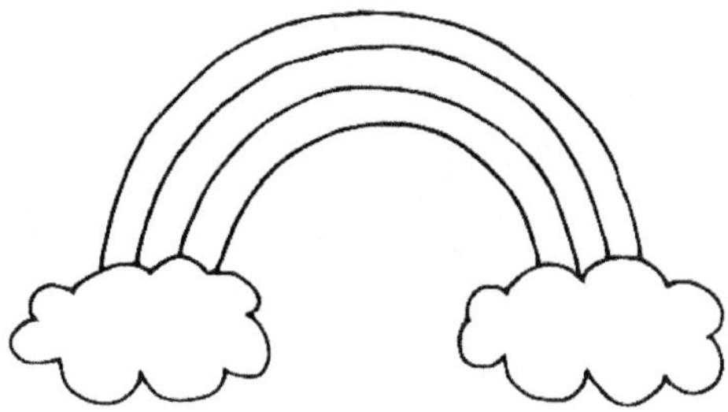

Chapter 3

Stolen Rainbow

"Well, Rosie, you have had many adventures for sure," Silvercrest said after Rosie told him about her last few months. "I wish Spark was here. I would love to meet him too."

"He should be back in a few days," said

Rosie. "How long will you and the Rainbow stay? And what is so special about the Sacred Rainbow, anyway?"

"The Sacred Rainbow is the power of the land and it powers the land too," the unicorn leader began. "It appears only once every year, in the middle of autumn,

when the land is getting ready for winter. The Rainbow draws power from all the elements of our beautiful land; from the ground

and stones, the

waters, the

plants and trees, the flowers and grasses, and the air and the

Sun. It stays here for about a week until it is full of the goodness the land needs. And then, the Rainbow releases the power back down to the ground, with a bit of magic added. It's a beautiful event to watch. You will love it, Rosie.

"Unfortunately, this magical and special event attracts creatures wanting to use the power the Rainbow gathers for evil. The

Rainbow holds so much power that we don't think there is anyone who could harness it, but that won't stop them from trying. It is crucial that the power goes back into the earth, otherwise the land will not thrive and might not survive the hard winter months."

Silvercrest looked at Rosie kindly, "It's the unicorns' duty to protect the Rainbow during this time. We've been its guardians for centuries."

Rosie listened intently. There was still so much about the land and the magical world that she didn't know, and she enjoyed learning about it.

For the rest of the day, Rosie played with Stardream, whose punishment wasn't too bad after all, and the time just flew. Rosie went home in the evening, happy and content, and ready for the next fun day.

In the morning, Rosie rushed to the window and her heart filled with dread. The Rainbow had gone!

Rosie shot out of the house, not even hearing her mum calling after her. She raced through the meadow and found the group of unicorns standing around the pond looking very upset.

"What happened? Where is the Rainbow?" Rosie blurted out.

"It's gone. It's been taken at night," whinnied Silvercrest sadly. "We must have been put under some sort of spell because none of us saw anything."

"Who could have taken it? And how?" asked Rosie.

Before the unicorns could answer, there was a silver tinkling sound and Queen Rosea, the ruler of the Rosula tree fairies, and her entourage arrived. She looked rather grim and solemn.

"I think I know who took the Rainbow," her voice rang. "We saw nothing last night, but the disturbance in the grass and in the forest points clearly at a large and clumsy creature. The song amongst the birds and animals is clear too. We think it was a troll."

Grave silence spread through the meadow. They all looked from one to another.

"What would a troll want with the Rainbow?" said Stardream. "It's not like that trolls can use its powers."

Silvercrest sighed, “I don’t think he wants to use its powers. He stole the Rainbow to take his revenge on us. We know the troll. His name is Ingens.”

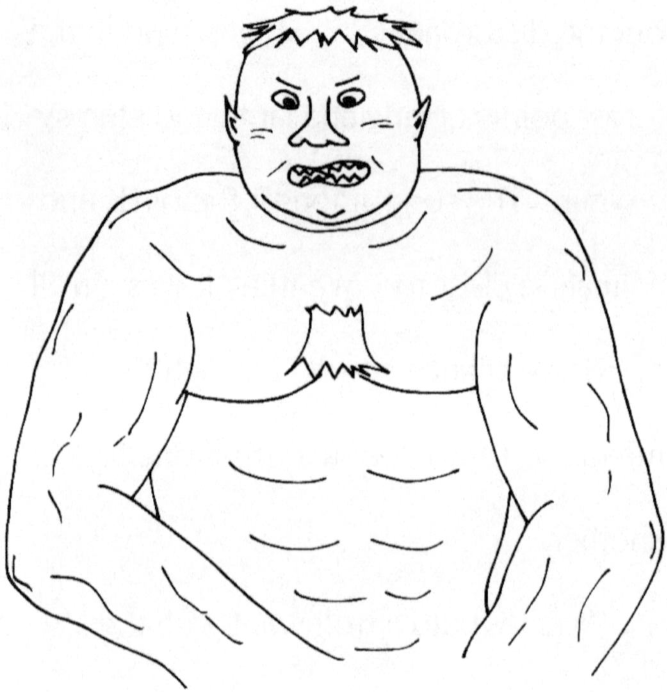

Chapter 4

Hide and Seek

Rosie watched the unicorns murmur and whinny. They all trembled at the sound of that name. It was certainly a name they feared.

“Who is Ingens?” asked Rosie.

Silvercrest looked at Rosie with deep

thoughts showing in his face. Then, as if he decided to share the story, he began.

"Ingens is an ancient troll who has been around for hundreds of years. Long before my time, Ingens befriended a young unicorn. It was such an unlikely friendship, and both the troll community and the unicorn herd frowned upon it. The unicorn's father, the mighty Golden Ray, forbade his son to continue this friendship. Ingens was devastated and promised to seek revenge on the unicorns. As the years passed, this promise turned into a bit of a myth. We scare our young ones with

Ingens when they misbehave, but nobody worries much about him anymore."

Silvercrest paused before continuing in a grave voice, "I guess he's finally figured out how to hurt us the most."

The meadow sunk into silence, broken only by the distant chirping of birds.

At last, Queen Rosea said, “If he doesn’t want the Rainbow for power, then we should be able to find where he hid it. Does anyone have any ideas?”

“Well…,” Rosie started bashfully. Everyone looked at her, waiting for her to go on.

“If I was hiding a rainbow,” continued Rosie, “I would separate the colours and camouflage them in places where they wouldn’t be visible.”

Rosie watched the fairies and unicorns processing this information.

“So, we just need to find something

colourful and the rainbow will be there?" blurted out Stardream. "I love playing hide and seek. This is going to be fun!"

"Stardream! This is not a game. This is a serious matter," growled Silvercrest.

"She is right, though. I think that's what we have to do. Let's at least try," pleaded Rosie.

Silvercrest's and Queen Rosea's eyes met and eventually they both nodded in agreement.

Stardream jumped in excitement, "So what is red? Where can we find red?"

They looked around, thinking. There

were trees with leaves turning red, a few late red meadow flowers and some red berries on bushes. Nothing was red enough to hide a whole band of red. Rosie could feel the motivation in the group dropping. Then she remembered where she saw a lot of red.

"When Spark and I walked through the woods, we came across a whole clearing full of young toadstools. You know, those red ones with white spots, the pretty ones. I bet now they are all fully opened."

"You mean fly agaric?" asked Queen Rosea.

“That would be them. Yes!” said Rosie.

“Lead the way, Rosie. We will follow,” commanded Silvercrest.

Rosie set off towards the trees. They walked past Spark's empty cave, further into the depths of the forest. It didn't take them long to arrive at the clearing. It was a large area with every space covered in red toadstools. There must have been thousands of them, sitting so close to each other that the ground was invisible and impassable.

Chapter 5

Mushroom Field

Rosie smiled, "This is absolutely beautiful. It's so much nicer than when we were here last time. Spark would love to see this."

The group of fairies zoomed above the clearing, checking around the mushrooms.

They came back in a hurry, talking at once. Queen Rosea quietened them. "What did you see?" she asked.

"The red strip is without doubt amongst the toadstools. It's weaved through the entire area," they said. "We cannot pick it up. It is too heavy for us."

"I can use my magic to do that," Queen Rosea said. She hovered in front of the clearing and murmured an incantation. With her hands moving from the bottom to the top, she raised her voice. Queen Rosea repeated the incantation several times, but nothing happened.

"I'm afraid, my magic is not powerful enough. There must be a spell on the Rainbow or the area. There's nothing I can do. I'm sorry," she sighed in despair.

"I can do it," peeped Rosie. "Can you find one of the ends? I'll just follow it and roll it up like a ribbon."

The fairies dashed away, soon finding both the ends. Rosie chose the one that was closer and, plucking up her courage, stepped into the mushroom field. She tried not to disturb the fungi too much, but they were so close together that it was impossible. Rosie hated the squishy softness underneath her feet, maybe even more than the way the caps brushed against her ankles and lower shins. Knowing that these toadstools were poisonous, she tried her best not to fall in.

At last, she reached the spot where the end was tucked in. Rosie picked it up, careful not to touch the mushrooms, and started winding it towards herself. This disturbed the toadstools, and a few of them pulled from the ground, revealing their gills, skirts, and stems. Rosie stopped. She didn't want to hurt the mushrooms more than necessary. It wasn't their fault.

Tiptoeing through the clearing, she rolled one bit at a time. This was an extremely tiring and time-consuming task. The roll in Rosie's hands kept on getting bigger and heavier, and with that, Rosie's body grew more tired. When she finally reached the end of the ribbon, Rosie rejoiced. She slipped out of the glade, plopping down on the ground, breathing a sigh of relief.

"You did it, Rosie. You were amazing," everyone cheered. Rosie smiled at them with happiness.

"The ribbon was so tightly wrapped around. I don't understand how the troll could have done that without spoiling the toadstools," said Rosie, puzzled.

"I believe the troll used magic. Where he got the powers from, I do not know," shrugged Queen Rosea. "He's put the unicorns under a spell first and now this. This matter will not be as easy as we thought, I'm afraid. Be on your guard, everyone, and expect the unexpected."

Chapter 6

Trouble with Pumpkins

Silvercrest nodded to one of his unicorns, who stepped forward. He asked Rosie to fasten the red bundle underneath the unicorn's belly for now.

While Rosie was wrapping it, Stardream was already bobbing up and down, thinking of possible orange objects. "There are leaves on the trees, orange flowers, maybe some foxes and squirrels in the forest. What else? What else is orange?"

A fairy ventured in a quiet voice, "There's the big pumpkin field just outside the forest, too."

"You are right," said Queen Rosea. "That would be the perfect place to hide the orange strip."

This time, they followed the fairies. They walked back to the meadow and headed away from the Redbud tree, the home of the Rosula tree fairies. It was easier to walk on the grass than force their way through the forest, especially for the unicorns. The journey was long, and after the toadstool incident, Rosie felt her body reaching its limit. Eventually, a large pumpkin patch came into view. As far as they could see, there were orange pumpkins.

Just like earlier, the fairies flew ahead, checking the whole patch for the orange Rainbow. They flew around frantically, but the ribbon was nowhere to be found. Rosie could see that the unicorns looked worried when a fairy shouted in the distance. The other fairies swooped towards her before flying back to the rest of the companions.

"The ribbon is there, but it is draped over and under the pumpkins," they reported.

"We can move the pumpkins and Rosie can roll up the ribbon again," Silvercrest decided.

The ground was quite wet after the recent rains and there were puddles in places. They trudged through the patch, arriving at the spot above which the fairies hovered. Some pumpkins there were so big that they reached to Rosie's knees.

They found the end of the strip with no issues and Rosie took hold of it. The unicorns had to work together to push the pumpkins away. They heaved with their heads and their bodies, slipping on the muddy ground. Stardream used her bum to bump into the smaller ones, moving them to the sides. Whenever she did that, she slipped in the mud afterwards. Soon, her body was almost covered in brown. She giggled and giggled and started falling on purpose, which amused the rest of the group.

Rosie kept on winding the ribbon until there was a full roll of it coiled in her hands. They all cheered and chatted happily while Rosie fastened the orange bundle on another unicorn. The Rainbow's magic kept the strip clean of mud, but the magic didn't work on them. They looked at each other and laughed.

"I think I will go home to have a wash,"

chuckled Rosie.

"That's a good idea, Rosie. Thank you for all your help. We couldn't have got the first two ribbons without you," said Silvercrest. "We can continue tomorrow; it's getting late now."

They walked back to the meadow where they said good night to each other and Rosie ran home.

Chapter 7

Where is Yellow?

Rosie could hardly wait for the next morning. She scoffed her breakfast and was off, leaving her mum shaking her head in disbelief. The holidays that Rosie thought were going to be dreadful turned to another exciting magical experience.

She just wished Spark was there with her to share the adventure.

The unicorns and fairies were already waiting for her. Everyone looked cheerful and full of anticipation for the new day. Rosie learnt that the unicorns safely stored the red and orange strips at the Rosula tree. The fairies' magic can protect them there until they find the rest of the Sacred Rainbow.

The next colour to search for was yellow. Ideas flowed through the group again. They saw yellow flowers in grass and yellow leaves on trees; some yellow apples hung in the apple trees. Yet, nothing seemed to be yellow enough.

"I know! I know!" shouted Stardream. "And Rosie too," she said, looking at Rosie. Rosie wasn't sure what she meant, so she just shook her head.

"Yes, you do. Remember when we were sliding down the Rainbow?" said Stardream.

"Sorry, Dad," she added when she noticed her father's disapproving glare.

"Far over the fields, was the bright yellow tree. You must have seen it, too. It was almost shining."

The realisation dawned on Rosie. She spotted a bright yellow spot in the distance, but in the exhilaration of sliding on a rainbow, she paid little attention to what it was.

"It's very far, Stardream. You think that the strip could be in that tree?" said Rosie.

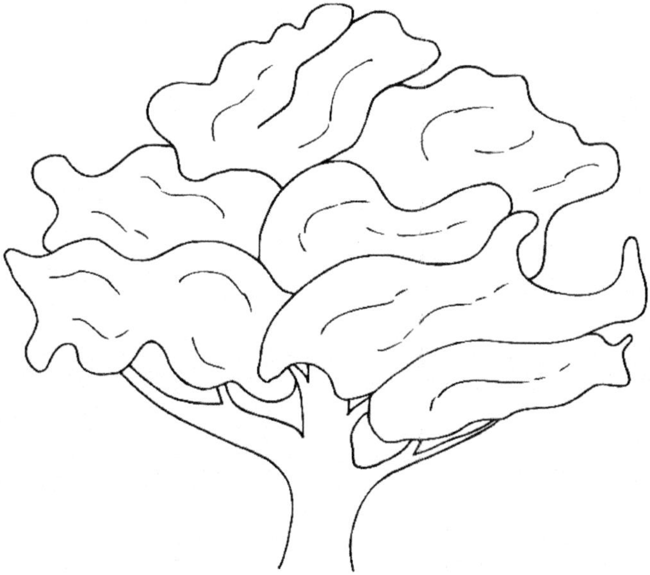

"It's the only bright yellow object around here, so it must be," insisted Stardream.

"We'll fly to have a look," offered the fairies. "Just show us the right direction."

Stardream and Rosie looked at each other.

"The Rainbow rose this way," nodded Rosie.

"And we slid from up there to here," mused Stardream.

"It must be this way!" they both pointed in the same direction, smiling in victory.

The fairies took off, disappearing from sight. The unicorns and Rosie waited on edge for their return. After what seemed like ages, but was really only a short time because fairies are fast flyers, a small swarm appeared in distance.

"They're back," whooped Stardream.

The fairies swooped down. They did find the tree and the yellow Rainbow band. However, the band was so well wrapped through the branches and leaves that they couldn't undo it. The entire group would have to journey to the tree.

"I can run with you, but it will take me

some time to get all the way there," said Rosie.

"You can ride on my back!" exclaimed Stardream.

"Stardream, you are too small and the journey would tire you too much. You are right, though, one of the unicorns can carry Rosie. If she accepts," Silvercrest looked expectantly at Rosie.

"I would love to," said Rosie. The thought of riding a unicorn was too thrilling.

Silvercrest beckoned to a stallion nearby who kneeled in front of Rosie, allowing her to mount him. Rosie hugged his neck tight with his beautiful white mane gently tickling her on her cheeks and neck. Then he rose and started walking with the rest of the herd.

Turning his head to Rosie, he said, "My

name is Snowmist. Hold on tight, we will gallop quite fast."

Rosie clutched his neck even tighter and with her heart beating wildly, they set off at a fast trot.

Chapter 8

Up the Tree

Rosie felt her body and mind relaxing. Riding a unicorn was sensational. She had ridden Spark many times, but only under water. The rush of wind in her hair and on her skin was a completely novel experience; and Rosie loved it. She watched the sharp gold-striped horn bobbing up and down in front of her. She smiled at the scenery passing by and secretly wished that this journey would never end.

In the distance in front of them, she could already see the yellow tree. The colour of the leaves was incredible. It was as if the Sun itself came down to the Earth to grace it with its beauty. It was a large tree, with wide branches stretching far into the sides and its crown high in the sky.

They arrived at the tree and Snowmist kneeled again for Rosie to dismount. She jumped into the golden foliage covering the ground and looked up into the tree.

The leaves swished and

rustled in the wind and the whole tree swayed. The view made her dizzy and Rosie had to sit down.

"Are you OK, Rosie?" worried Stardream.

"Yes, I am. My head is just spinning a bit," said Rosie.

"Maybe after the ride."

Stardream nudged her with her nose affectionately.

In the meantime, the fairies flew around the tree, looking for the end of the yellow band. They returned to the group of unicorns after finding it.

"We found the end, but none of us can undo it. It's wound around the maple trunk," said Queen Rosea. "Rosie, how well can you climb?"

Rosie looked at Queen Rosea in alarm. She wanted her to climb up that enormous tree?!

"Hmm…," she stammered, "I guess I can try it."

With shaky legs, Rosie stood up. She walked to the maple tree and tried to reach the bottom branch. It was too high. Snowmist hurried to her side, and just like before, kneeled, inviting her to climb onto his back. Rosie clambered on. The branch was within her reach now, but still too high. She realised she would have to stand up. Taking a strong hold of the branch, she drew up. Her legs shook like jelly, but Rosie managed to pull her body up onto the branch. She threw one leg over, straightened her body, and sat up. Then she inched her way towards the trunk, hugging it.

The fairies flew around her, encouraging her every move.

Rosie smiled at them and rose to her full height. Another branch was not far away. With little effort, Rosie climbed up that branch, finding the next one even closer. The maple tree had so many branches that climbing up it proved to be easier than she had expected. She reached the end of the yellow strip in no time at all.

Rosie sat down, straddling the branch

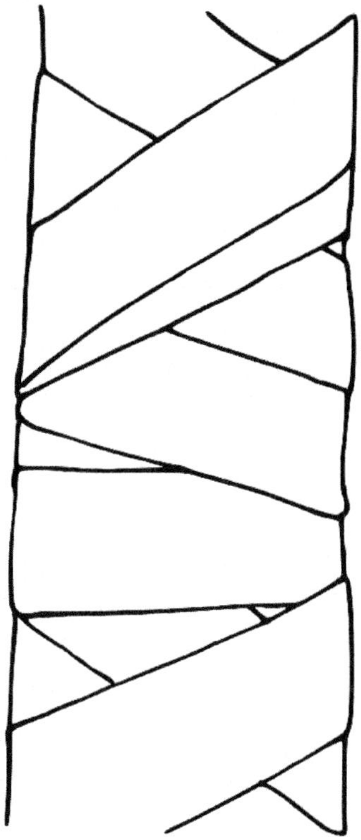

with her legs, and untied the ending. She passed it to the fairies, who flew around the trunk many times, freeing the band. Soon yellow colour was everywhere. Rosie got hold of the end and started winding it up. The roll in her hands bulked up, but there was still more stuck around the tree.

"Rosie, can you try climbing higher,

please?" asked Queen Rosea.

Rosie tucked the roll in her top and pulled her body upwards. The higher she climbed, the slimmer the trunk became. When she got to the spot where the ribbon was still wrapped, she could touch her fingers around the trunk. Pulling the roll out, she passed the bundle around the tree while rolling more of the strip on.

To reach the end, she had to climb even higher. She swallowed hard as the trunk swayed from side to side. Rosie worked fast. With the last bit secured on the roll, she stored it underneath her top again and started her descent. She was about halfway down when she slipped and fell.

Chapter 9

Into the Swamp

At the last second, Rosie gripped a branch with her arms. She hung off, breathing hard.

"Rosie, there's a branch right beside your foot," chirped a fairy in her ear. "I'm sure you can reach it."

Rosie looked down and spotted the branch. She stretched her leg towards it, stepping on. Sighing

with relief, she transferred her weight onto it and moved her second leg to the branch, too. She then walked to the trunk, still holding onto the branch above. She hugged the trunk for a while before continuing her way down.

Snowmist was waiting for her under the tree. Rosie lowered her body onto his and hugged the large unicorn in relief.

"Thank you," Rosie whispered in his ear

before hopping off.

The entire group circled Rosie, hugging her and cheering.

"Rosie, you were brilliant!" cried Stardream. "Just brilliant!"

"It's time to go back, everyone. We still have a lot of work to do," called Silvercrest to quieten them.

"Where could the green Rainbow be?" mused the fairies when they returned to the pond.

"Everything around is green, so it's

hard to say," said a unicorn mare.

Queen Rosea hovered above all. "Fairies, fly around the forest, fields and meadows. Fly high and low and watch for anything that is out of ordinary, anything that shouldn't be." The fairies hastened away, while the unicorns took the yellow ribbon to the safety of the Rosula tree.

One by one, the fairies started returning. The news was not positive. Nothing out of ordinary seemed to be present in the area. Then a small fairy came back full of excitement.

"There's a green mound in the middle

of the Loggy swamp. I'm sure I haven't seen it there before," exclaimed the fairy.

"Lead the way," ordered Silvercrest. The group followed the fairy into the forest.

Rosie and Spark explored the forest all the time. She knew the swamp the fairy talked about. It was a boggy and dreary place with lots of logs fallen into the mud. The forest around was dark, with tall trees blocking the light almost completely. Rosie didn't like that place.

As they walked deeper into the forest, their feelings fell, too. The growing dampness around them dispirited them all.

When they arrived at the swamp, the companions' mood lifted. In the middle stood a bright green hill, so bright that the surrounding air shone. They were in the right place.

The fairies flew to the mound and tried lifting it up. However, even when they all worked together, they couldn't. Rosie knew she would have to do it.

"I think I could jump across using the logs," ventured Rosie.

The unicorns looked at her with affection and Silvercrest said, "They will be slippery, Rosie. Are you sure?"

"Yes, I'll give it a go," said Rosie with resolution.

She took her shoes off and stepped on the first log. She felt the spongy moss with her feet. The logs were slippery and Rosie had to use her hands to keep her balance. Slowly but steadily, she moved along. The swamp was full of logs and Rosie had no problems finding her way. She drew nearer and nearer to the mound and not long after setting off, she jumped on it.

The softness of the surface surprised her, and her body sank inside.

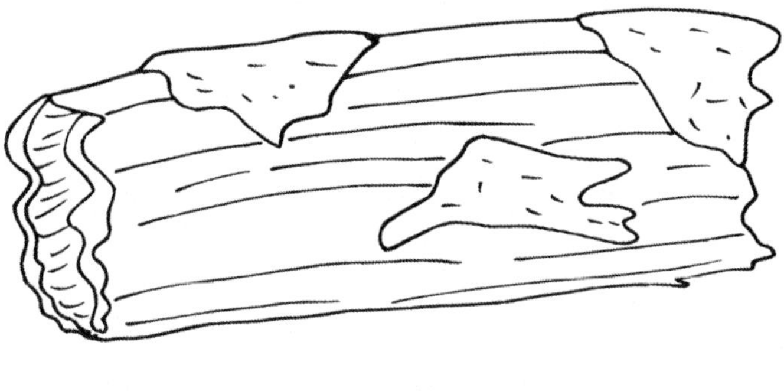

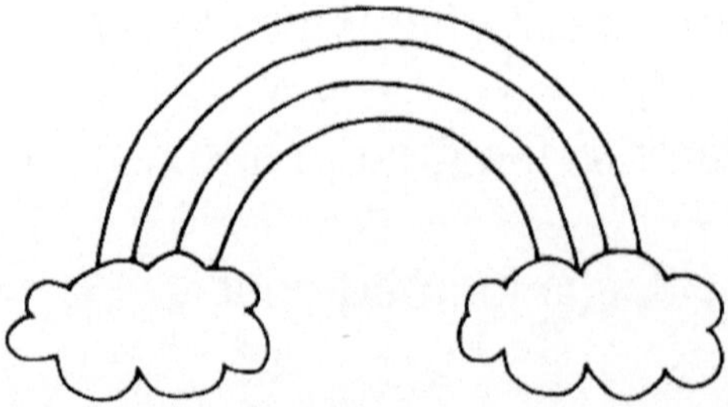

Chapter 10

Time for a Swim

Rosie's feet hit something boggy but solid. She was standing on a muddy log with the green band surrounding her. Regaining her awareness, she searched for the end. The fairies fluttered around, helping.

“Here it is,” exclaimed one, giving the end to Rosie who begun rolling it up.

The hill grew smaller and smaller until it was gone and Rosie had her hands full. She didn’t understand how that mound could be all in this roll. The troll must have used magic for sure.

With the roll underneath her top, Rosie made her way to the unicorns.

“Well, this was fun,” smiled Rosie at Stardream.

Turning to Silvercrest she added, “I will have to go home now. I’m afraid it’s getting late and I could use a bath, too.”

The leader nodded and whinnied.

Rosie sprinted through the house in the morning, grabbing her breakfast and disappearing. She grinned at her mum, who was shaking her head. Mum asked her the night before what she did the whole day. Rosie knew that telling the truth was the best idea, so she said she had played with unicorns and fairies. Mum mumbled something about her great imagination and left her to it. Just as Rosie had expected.

The unicorns were waiting for her

already, discussing the possibilities for the blue ribbon's hiding spots. They all agreed that the only logical place would be water. The fairies had left earlier to search the area, and now, one by one, they were returning. None with good news. They had checked every single body of water in the area with no luck.

Queen Rosea and Silvercrest had their heads together, and Stardream kicked a little pebble around. The other unicorns munched on some grass, and the fairies rested on the ground. Rosie walked back and forth, thinking. She wandered to the little pond. The water was clear and bright blue. Rosie kneeled at the edge, wanting to try how cool it was. She looked in and saw something shimmering at the bottom.

"Has anyone checked this pond?" she called to the group, excitement growing in her body.

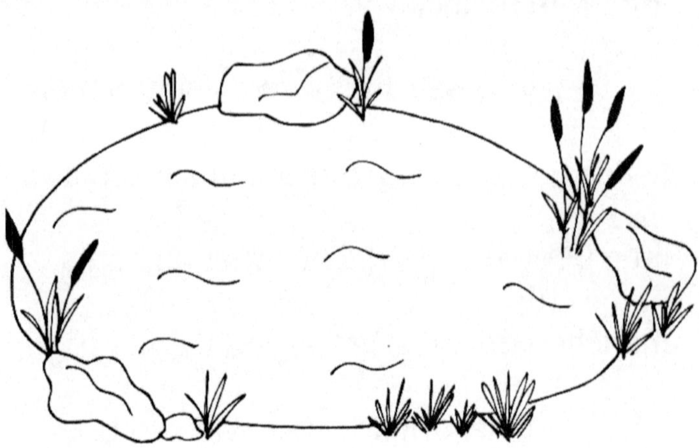

Everyone rushed to her and crowded the sides. Queen Rosea hovered above the surface and exclaimed, “It is down there! Look!”

“It’s been here all along,” smiled Silvercrest.

“How are we going to get the Rainbow out?” ventured Stardream. “Unicorns can’t swim under water and fairies neither.”

They all looked at Rosie, who already knew what was coming.

“I will do it,” said Rosie, smiling.

She took her clothes off, and dressed only in her underwear, tested the water.

Goosebumps sprang all over her body straight away, and she shivered. Rosie felt comfortable in water and so she took a big breath and plunged in. Her body recovered from the chilly shock fast and, with her eyes on the prize, she dived into the pond.

The pond was deeper than it looked,

but at last Rosie reached the bottom. She grasped the ribbon and started pulling it behind her. With the wet and heavy band, swimming proved to be a challenging task.

Rosie heaved with all her strength while kicking her feet. The surface got closer and then Rosie bobbed above it, taking a deep, much needed breath. Swimming to the edge, she passed the band to the unicorns, who pulled the total length out of the pond. Rosie climbed out of the water, shivering with cold. She picked up her clothes to get dressed when a vast shadow covered the Sun and something swooped down. The unicorns whinnied in panic and pelted across the meadow.

Chapter 11

Dark Cave

Rosie knew that shadow very well.

Rejoicing, she ran towards the creature.

"Spark! You're back!" shouted Rosie, hugging her friend.

Spark trembled with happiness and

folded his wings around her. When they peeled from each other, Spark growled at Rosie.

"Yes, I've been swimming," she laughed.

Without further hesitation, Spark blew his warm dragon breath at Rosie until she was dry.

"Thank you. That's what I needed," she smiled at him.

Rosie looked around at the unicorns clopping back to the pond.

"Everyone, this is Spark," said Rosie, giving Spark another hug. "And Spark, this is Silvercrest and his unicorn herd. I've been helping them to find the Sacred Rainbow."

Spark looked at her eagerly.

"I'll explain everything later," assured him Rosie, "but now, can you please dry this blue ribbon?"

Spark puffed a gentle, warm gust of air all over the blue band. Rosie then wound it up and, while carrying it to the fairy tree, filled Spark in on everything.

"So, next we will search for the indigo ribbon," concluded Rosie.

"That's right," said Silvercrest. "Does anyone have any ideas where the indigo could be?"

"It will be a dark place," whickered

Stardream.

Spark grunted at Rosie.

"Spark says that his cave is dark," said Rosie.

"Of course! A cave would be the best spot," said Silvercrest. "Could you please look in your cave?"

Spark nodded and took off towards the forest, his great wings beating the air.

"Spark gave us such a fright," admitted Silvercrest, with the other unicorns dipping their heads in agreement.

The dragon came back in no time, shaking his head. He found nothing.

"The only other cave around here is the one we found Spark in," added Queen Rosea in a quiet voice.

Rosie knew Queen Rosea still grieved her sister and going back to the cave where she defeated her would be hard. However, the Queen understood the Rainbow was too important and so she organised her fairies and they were off. The unicorns and Rosie with Spark followed them.

They arrived at the cave. Spark and the unicorns were too big to go in and so Rosie and the fairies proceeded on their own. It was as if the time turned back half a year. The cave looked the same, but the passages seemed narrower than Rosie had remembered. She must have grown!

They searched every little opening and every dark corner for the ribbon. There was nothing. Then, from the corner of her eye, Rosie spotted a spiderweb hanging low from the ceiling. Only the spiderweb was a bit too dense. Rosie pointed it to the fairies, who flew up to inspect it. They cheered; it was the end of the indigo Rainbow strip. They brought it towards Rosie, who pulled it down piece by piece.

In the time the strip had been there, some spiders made it their home. Now they were falling around Rosie, some even crawling up her legs and arms.

Rosie wasn't afraid of spiders, but she didn't like them on her. She dropped the ball of indigo and brushed them off her body. The fairies laughed and promised to keep the spiders away.

Rosie rolled the strip up and they set off on the journey back. They were almost out when they heard strange noises coming from outside.

"You meddling unicorns and fairies," the voice gnarled, "Me show you!"

And with that, a large boulder blocked the exit of the cave. Rosie and the fairies were trapped.

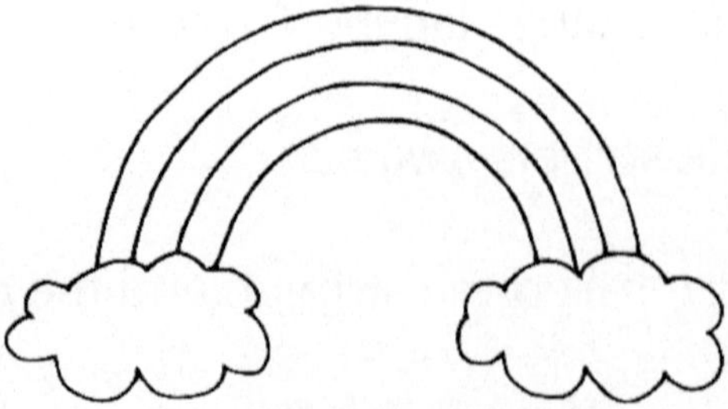

Chapter 12

Ingens Explains

Queen Rosea didn't delay. She asked five fairies to stay with Rosie, and the rest flew with her to the top cavern. They knew there was a way out.

In the meantime, Rosie listened to the happenings outside.

"You think you will stop Ingens?" shrieked the voice. "You won't!"

Then there was a loud growl and an enormous thud. For a while, silence spread everywhere; until Queen Rosea's voice rang through the clearing.

"Leave my friends alone," she cried.

Huge sobs filled the air. "Friends? What about Ingens? Who Ingens friend?"

The creature was sobbing, visibly in deep despair. Rosie heard a long, soft growl. She recognised Spark; and she understood what he was saying. He was offering to be Ingens's friend.

Then the boulder moved. When there was a gap large enough, Spark's nose appeared in it. He snorted and Rosie kissed him. She followed him outside and stopped in her tracks.

There, in the middle of the clearing, stood a large troll. His body was like a stone in appearance, but shaped like a man. Spark nudged her, grunting. Rosie plucked up her courage and, on shaky legs, stepped forward.

"Nice to meet you," she said. "My name is Rosie."

The troll screwed up his face in

something that must have been a smile and said, "Me Ingens, you dragon friend."

"Ingens sorry. Ingens caused lot of trouble." The troll looked sheepishly at Rosie.

"Dragon friend forgive Ingens?"

Rosie grinned. Ingens was funny. "It's not my place to forgive you, Ingens," she said. “The unicorns are the Sacred Rainbow’s guardians.”

Ingens turned to the unicorns, “Ingens wanted friend. Ingens got angry and spoiled unicorn rainbow.”

Silvercrest stepped forward. “I speak for all the unicorns and we do forgive you, Ingens. It was our forefather who wronged you. Can you forgive us too, please?”

Ingens nodded with surprise and beamed at them.

“I have a question,” said Queen Rosea. “You used powerful magic. Where did it come from?”

"Ingens met fairy. Fairy promised Ingens power if Ingens build a cave for her. Ingens very good at caves," the troll praised himself, patting his chest with one hand and pointing at the cave behind them with the other.

"You built this cave?" asked Rosie.

"Ingens very clever. Ingens built good cave! Strong, deep, and dark. Perfect cave," he nodded. "And then fairy wanted dragon. Ingens took egg from dragon nest and gave it to fairy. Fairy then gave Ingens red ball. Ingens threw ball at rainbow and rainbow flew away. Ingens sorry."

Ingens hung his head low, shuffling his feet with soft clangs.

"Noctis!" breathed Queen Rosea, realising her sister was behind this. "That explains why my magic doesn't work on the Rainbow. Even now, Noctis's dark magic is stronger. She had grown extremely powerful."

Everyone in the clearing sunk into an uneasy silence until Silvercrest broke it. "We need to find the last band; we're still missing violet."

"Has anyone seen anything purple on their travels?" said Rosie.

Spark nudged her and grunted, swishing his tail from side to side.

"You know where, Spark? Tell us!" pressed Rosie. Spark rose towards the sky, growling at the group.

"He wants us to follow him," said

Rosie.

"We will go with him first," said Queen Rosea before taking off with the fairies.

Rosie, the unicorns and Ingens waited in the clearing. They didn't need to wait long when Spark and the fairies returned.

"There's a huge lavender field behind the forest. It must be a very late crop, but it's in full bloom. The violet strip is woven through one row of plants."

"Wonderful, let's go then!" commanded Silvercrest.

Chapter 13

Rainbow Returns

To be faster, Rosie mounted Snowmist again, and they followed the fairies through the forest. After some time, the trees grew sparse and their view opened to a purple field. A sweet scent drifted to them on the breeze and the loud buzzing of bees, collecting pollen and nectar, was almost deafening.

"The strip's end is over there," said Queen Rosea, pointing at one row of lavender plants. They saw that the colour of that row was different, a shade pinker than the rest of the field.

"Rosie, can you help to get the band and roll it up again?" asked Silvercrest.

Rosie nodded and walked into the field. Straight away, a couple of bees circled her and one stung her arm.

"Ouch!" cried Rosie, backing out of the field again.

Queen Rosea rushed to her, "I will heal you, Rosie." She then blew on the sting and recited a short verse. The pain from Rosie's arm disappeared and the redness around the sting subsided.

"Thank you," said Rosie. "I don't think I'll be able to get the violet band. There are too many bees."

"I believe we can help with that," chimed the Queen. "Bees are our friends. We can fly with you and protect you from them."

Queen Rosea assembled her fairies around Rosie and then entered the field, singing words that Rosie didn't understand. The bees did, however, and none came close to Rosie again.

Rosie found the end of the strip. She unwound it from the plant and started rolling it up. She continued doing so until she had the whole violet Rainbow bundled up in her hands. Smiling, she carried it back to the unicorns.

Everyone cheered with delight. They had found all the pieces of the Sacred Rainbow. The time has come to put them back together.

Once they reached the Redbud tree, they carried the pieces out. They spread them on the grass in the correct order, with one end of each colour dipped in the pond. The moment all the pieces were down, the strips began to move. They attached itself to each other, creating one

colourful band.

The band floated up to the sky and stretched from the water's surface across the forest.

Rosie heard Queen Rosea sigh with relief. She glanced at her. The Queen noticed and whispered, "I was worried the magic would still be too strong for the Rainbow. I'm glad the power of the land was superior."

Loud cheers rang through the meadow. The unicorns dashed around, whinnying and jumping in delight. Stardream couldn't help herself, climbed up the Rainbow, and slid down. Her father rolled his eyes but said nothing. Stardream winked at Rosie, who laughed.

Everyone was overjoyed. Even Ingens, who caused all the trouble, bounced up and down. The ground shook with his loud yowls and howls.

The Sacred Rainbow was back where it belonged.

Chapter 14

Sight to Remember

Rosie lay in bed that night, thinking of all the adventures that she had had with the unicorns. She could hardly wait for the next day. Silvercrest said that the Rainbow seemed almost ripe. Being separate and positioned in the land and its elements had helped it to draw the goodness in much faster. Tomorrow it will send the power, with some rainbow magic, back into the land. And that was a sight to remember.

Rosie rolled from one side of the bed to the other, too excited to sleep. At last, she drifted to the land of dreams with colours swirling through her mind.

Just like the morning before, Rosie sprinted out of the house, barely eating her breakfast. The Rainbow was still there, its colours more vivid than before. It seemed bigger and wider and jittered in the still air.

Everyone gathered underneath it. Spark sniffed Rosie to greet her, and Ingens hollered in his loud voice, "Morning, dragon friend!"

"Here you are, Rosie. Right on time," said Silvercrest. "The Sacred Rainbow is almost ready. Watch!"

Rosie looked up at the Rainbow. It trembled with its colours growing brighter and plumper every minute. The colours grew so round that they were almost bursting up at seams. Little multi-coloured flashes zoomed all around it. When Rosie thought the Rainbow couldn't get any more

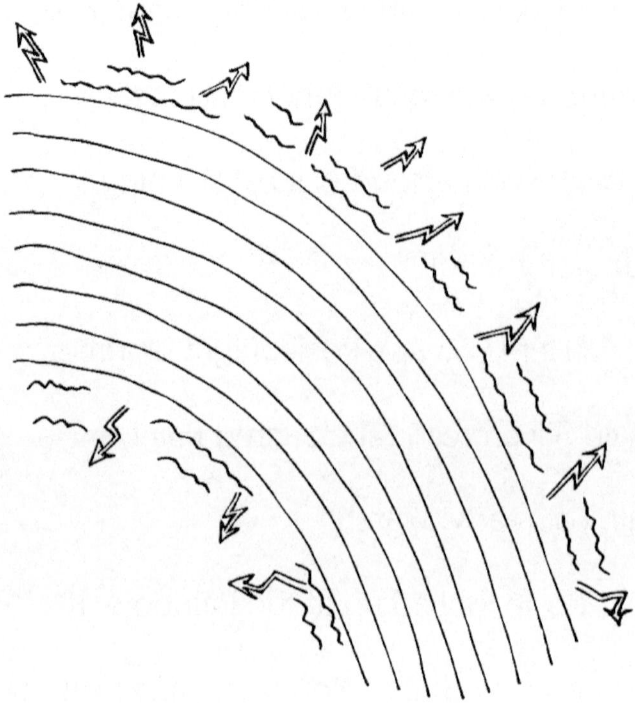

magnificent, a loud boom split the air. The ground quaked and the surrounding grass turned rainbow. The Sacred Rainbow was dispersing its power back into the land.

Rosie's mouth dropped in awe. The

world around her took on hues of the Rainbow. Not only the grass, but the trees, plants and everything around turned rainbow-like. The Sacred Rainbow kept on pumping all the collected goodness into the pond, growing lighter as the colours left it.

Spark grunted at Rosie. She looked at him in surprise. "You want me to fly up with you?"

He nodded. Rosie mounted Spark's back and clutched his neck. The spikes were uncomfortable, but she was determined to hold on. Spark soared up with care. Rosie closed her eyes for a moment. She wasn't sure that she wanted to see the ground moving away. When she opened them again, she gasped at the beauty underneath her. The rainbow colours were coursing through the land. Far on the horizon, Rosie followed the scenery changing. Soon, as far as she could see, were only red, orange, yellow, green, blue, indigo, and violet shades.

Rosie looked for The Sacred Rainbow. It disappeared from the autumn sky, with the last drops of goodness just sinking into the pond. Rosie noticed the natural colours returning to the land below her and the last of the Rainbow fading in the distance.

The Earth was full of new power and strong again, ready for the harsh months ahead.

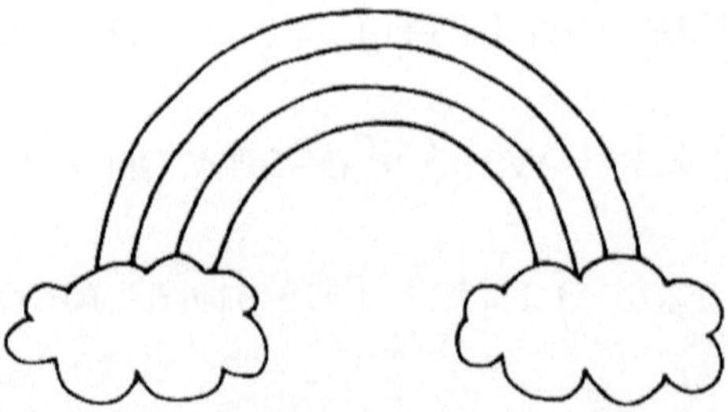

Chapter 15

Farewell to Friends

"This was amazing, Spark. Thank you very much. I loved seeing it from the top," said Rosie to Spark after he landed back on the ground.

"What happens now?" asked Rosie the unicorn leader.

"Our job here is done for now," Silvercrest replied. "We will go home. But we will be back next year to guard the new Sacred Rainbow."

Rosie's heart hurt. She had become fond of the unicorns, especially little Stardream.

Stardream looked upset, too. She wasn't ready to say goodbye to her new friend. Rosie hugged her neck and buried her face in the mane.

"I will see you next year, Stardream. I will miss you."

Stardream whinnied tearfully before galloping to join her father and the other unicorns. The rest of the group watched them go until the unicorns disappeared from view. Spark flew up and accompanied them for a bit.

"What are you going to do, Ingens?" asked Rosie the troll.

"Ingens stay with Spark for a bit, dragon friend. If you okay with it."

"Of course, I am! Spark does get lonely when I'm not around," said Rosie.

Then she continued, "I wanted to ask you something. You said that you brought Noctis a dragon egg."

"Ingens did. Ingens went to Murky Peak and took one. Ingens clever, dragon didn't see Ingens."

"I think Spark is the egg, Ingens!" said Rosie, letting the information sink in.

Ingens's mouth opened wide. He gaped at Rosie in disbelief.

"Would you find the dragon nest again, Ingens? I would like to help Spark find his family."

"Ingens would. Ingens know exactly where it is. Ingens help," he shook his head with vigour.

"Thank you, Ingens. I will talk to Spark first," added Rosie, looking at the sky where Spark was returning to them.

Queen Rosea approached Rosie. "Thank you again for your help, Rosie. Our Book of Lore was correct. You have become a great protector of the enchanted realms. I don't know what we would have done without you."

Rosie blushed at this praise and curtsied to the Queen. The fairies bowed and fluttered to their tree.

Rosie, Spark and Ingens were left alone. All of a sudden, the meadow was empty and quiet. After the hive of activity of the previous days, this was a tremendous change. Rosie loved her adventure and making new friends, but both her body and mind felt exhausted after the perilous events. She was ready for a calm ending to her school holidays.

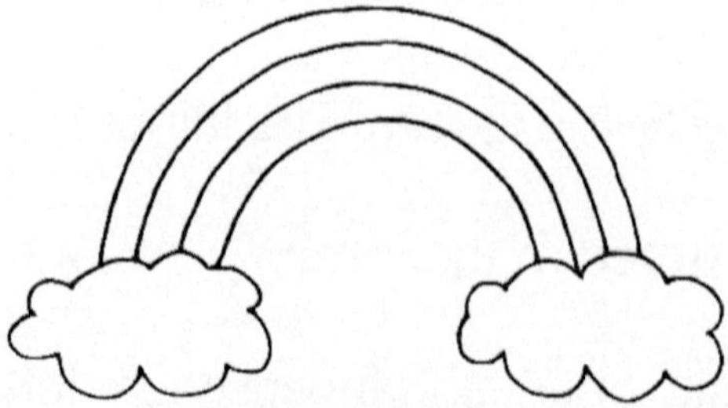

Epilogue

Rosie and Spark sat in front of his cave. Spark was unusually quiet. Rosie guessed what Spark was wondering about.

"Spark, did you hear Ingens talking about the dragon egg?" she said, observing Spark's behaviour.

Spark looked at her with sadness and a low growl.

"I figured you realised it was you. What are you going to do?"

With affection, the dragon nuzzled Rosie and puffed. Rosie understood he tried to tell her he had everything he needed right there. She wished it to be true, but in her heart of hearts, she knew it wasn't. He needed his family as much as she needed hers.

With a lump in her throat, she said, "I spoke to Ingens. He remembers where he took the egg from. He could take us there.

What do you think, Spark? Would you like to find your family?"

Spark's expression changed to that of pure joy. He pushed Rosie over and licked her entire face. Rosie laughed and laughed.

She had her answer.

Their next adventure was crystal clear.

The End

Now you've enjoyed **Unicorn Mission**, check out other books by Iveta Ongley.

Picture books:

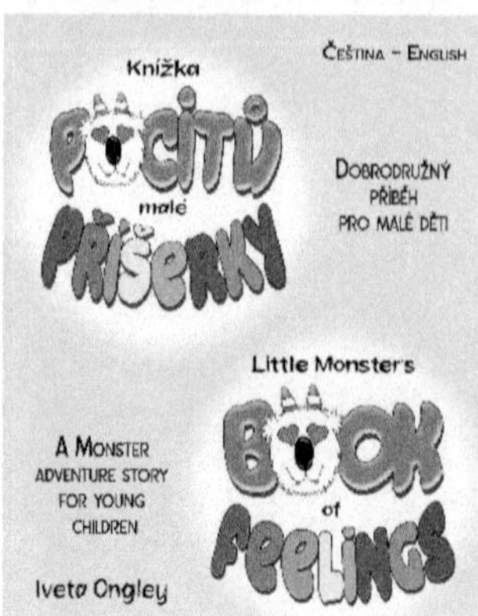

Chapter books:

For an updated selection visit
www.ivetaongley.co.nz

I love to read reviews and hear your suggestions and feedback.
Please, consider leaving one for **Unicorn Mission** on my website and Amazon by following the QR codes below:

Website

Amazon

About the Author and Illustrator

Iveta Ongley

was born in the Czech Republic and as a child loved pretending being a teacher, only to grow up to become one. Her love of reading was enticed by her dad, who would spend uncountable hours with his nose buried in books.

After meeting her husband when working in New Zealand, she settled in the beautiful country. They live in Auckland with their two daughters and two cats. She finds inspiration for her books in her children but they are also the greatest and most gorgeous distraction from writing.

www.ivetaongley.co.nz
Facebook: @ivetaongleyauthor
Instagram: #ivetawrites

Printed in Great Britain
by Amazon

29237455R00076